I WANT to BE in a SCARY STORY

Sean Taylor

For dancing Rob – S.T.

Jean Jullien

For Lou – J.J.

WALKER BOOKS
AND SUBSIDIARIES
LONDON · BOSTON · SYDNEY · AUCKLAND

First published 2017 by Walker Books Ltd, 87 Vauxhall Walk, London SE11 5HJ • Text © 2017 Sean Taylor • Illustrations © 2017 Jean Jullien • The right of Sean Taylor and Jean Jullien to be identified as author and illustrator respectively of this work has been asserted by them in accordance with the Copyright, Designs and Patents Act 1988 • This book has been typeset in URW Egyptienne T and Futura Bold • Printed in China • All rights reserved. No part of this book may be reproduced, transmitted or stored in an information retrieval system in any form or by any means, graphic, electronic or mechanical, including photocopying, taping and recording, without prior written permission from the publisher. • British Library Cataloguing in Publication Data: a catalogue record for this book is available from the British Library • ISBN 978-1-4063-6346-3 • www.walker.co.uk • 10 9 8 7 6 5 4 3 2

MIX
Paper from
responsible sources
FSC® C008047

Hello, Little Monster.

What do you want to do today?

Can I be in a story?

All right. What sort of story?

I want to be in a SCARY story!

A *funny* story might be more fun.

Not for me it won't be!

OK. We could start the story in
a dark and scary forest.

That's a good idea.

You ready then, Little Monster?

You bet I am!

Is that too scary?

It MIGHT be.

Would you rather
it was just a
spooky house?

That sounds better!

Is that *too* spooky?

A little bit.
But never mind.

Well, now something scary
is going to happen.

What?

You go inside,
and a creepy witch
will jump out.

OK.

Would you rather
something else jumped out,
instead of the witch?

Maybe.

How about a ghost?

OK.
A ghost.

HOLD ON! This is too scary!

Well, you did say you wanted to be in a scary story.

I know. But...
I want to be in a scary story where *I* do the scaring!

Oh, *you* want to be the scary one?

YEAH!

OK then. You can creep up the stairs, sneak over to the door and then ...
SCARE THE PERSON INSIDE!

All right!

Wait a moment...

Who is going to be in there?

The witch.

WHAT?

Look, can't we maybe change
this book so it's a FUNNY story?!

All right, Little Monster.
There could be just a
teeny weeny monkey
and his friend
in there.

Good! That's going to be much funnier and better!

It's not fair if his friend's GINORMOUS like that!

But you said you want this to be a FUNNY story now, didn't you?

Yes...

Well, it's going to be funny if a ginormous monkey and a teeny weeny monkey start chasing a monster, isn't it?

Not for me
it won't be!

Unless... what? Hey, Little

Monster! Are you OK?

Little
Monster?

Are you
out here?

The
forest is
dark and
scary!

Now that WAS scary,
Little Monster!

And that was
FUNNY, too!

So, can I be in a story again tomorrow?